A Note to Parents and Caregivers:

Read-it! Readers are for children who are just starting on the amazing road to reading. These beautiful books support both the acquisition of reading skills and the love of books.

The PURPLE LEVEL presents basic topics and objects using high frequency words and simple language patterns.

The RED LEVEL presents familiar topics using common words and repeating sentence patterns.

The BLUE LEVEL presents new ideas using a larger vocabulary and varied sentence structure.

The YELLOW LEVEL presents more challenging ideas, a broad vocabulary, and wide variety in sentence structure.

The GREEN LEVEL presents more complex ideas, an extended vocabulary range, and expanded language structures.

The ORANGE LEVEL presents a wide range of ideas and concepts using challenging vocabulary and complex language structures.

When sharing a book with your child, read in short stretches, pausing often to talk about the pictures. Have your child turn the pages and point to the pictures and familiar words. And be sure to reread favorite stories or parts of stories.

There is no right or wrong way to share books with children. Find time to read with your child, and pass on the legacy of literacy.

Adria F. Klein, Ph.D.
Professor Emeritus
California State University
San Bernardino, California

Editors: Christianne Jones and Dodie Marie Miller
Designer: Amy Muehlenhardt
Page Production: Brandie Shoemaker
Art Director: Nathan Gassman
The illustrations in this book were created digitally.

Picture Window Books
5115 Excelsior Boulevard
Suite 232
Minneapolis, MN 55416
877-845-8392
www.picturewindowbooks.com

Printed in the United States of America.

Library of Congress Cataloging-in-Publication Data
Anderson, Joseph P. (Joseph Patrick), 1982-
The kickball game / by Joseph P. Anderson ; illustrated by Justin Greathouse.
p. cm. — (Read-it! readers)
Summary: During a game of kickball, Danny thinks he has made a horrible mistake,
but Jenny shows him the humorous side of what he did.
ISBN-13: 978-1-4048-2413-3 (library binding)
ISBN-10: 1-4048-2413-8 (library binding)
ISBN-13: 978-1-4048-2443-0 (paperback)
ISBN-10: 1-4048-2443-X (paperback)
[1. Friendship—Fiction. 2. Sports—Fiction. 3. Winning and losing—Fiction.]
I. Greathouse, Justin, 1981- ill. II. Title.
PZ7.A5376Ki 2006
[E]—dc22
                                         2006027285

The Kickball Game

by Joseph P. Anderson

illustrated by Justin Greathouse

Special thanks to our advisers for their expertise:

Adria F. Klein, Ph.D.
Professor Emeritus, California State University
San Bernardino, California

Susan Kesselring, M.A.
Literacy Educator
Rosemount–Apple Valley–Eagan (Minnesota) School District

Hi! My name is Danny.

This is my best friend, Jenny.

We met in gym class.

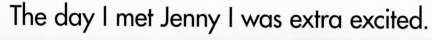

The day I met Jenny I was extra excited.
It was kickball day.

8

Kickball is my favorite sport.

When it was my turn to kick, I was ready.

The gym teacher rolled the perfect pitch.

But when I went to kick the ball, something embarrassing happened. I had forgotten to tie my shoe, and it flew off.

My shoe went farther than the
ball did! The center fielder, Nicole,
caught it.

I didn't know what to do, so I ran to first base. Nicole threw my shoe to Jenny, who was playing first base.

I was embarrassed that my shoe had flown off. I almost started crying.

Jenny whispered something to me.

While everyone was playing with my shoe, the ball kept rolling.

Jenny told me to keep running. I made it all the way to home base!

I had kicked a home run! Instead of being embarrassed, I was proud. My team won the game.

21

Now, Jenny and I eat lunch together every day.

She always reminds me to tie my shoes.

We are best friends.

More *Read-it!* Readers

Bright pictures and fun stories help you practice your reading skills. Look for more books at your level.

Bears on Ice
The Bossy Rooster
The Camping Scare
Dust Bunnies
Emily's Pictures
Flying with Oliver
Frog Pajama Party
Galen's Camera
Greg Gets a Hint
Last in Line
The Lifeguard
Mike's Night-light
Nate the Dinosaur
One Up for Brad
Robin's New Glasses
The Sassy Monkey
The Treasure Map
Tuckerbean
What's Bugging Pamela?

Looking for a specific title or level? A complete list of Read-it! Readers is available on our Web site:
www.picturewindowbooks.com